# TAUGHT A LESSON

THE NARDONE FAMILY SAGA

LIA RAE

Taught A Lesson



This book contains sexually explicit material and scenes of a non-consensual nature which is suitable only for mature readers and may be upsetting if this is a trigger for you. Please do not read this book in that case

www.authorliarae.com

Created with Vellum

## ALSO BY LIA RAE

**Bound Clubs Novels**

Chicago Bound

Atlanta Bound

Paradise Bound

Bound to Be Found

**The Nardone Family Saga**

Bought and Paid For

Caught In the Act

Sought After

Taught a Lesson

Four Weddings at Christmas

**Ranger Valley Ranch Adventures**

The Ranger's Fake Bride

Rescued by the Ranger

The Ranger's Baby

The Ranger's Nanny

# ONE

The bar was absolutely packed. Granted, it was only the third full weekend it had been open, but Vince couldn't wrap his head around the number of people packed into the place. *Bevanda* was the newest acquisition of Gemini Incorporated, the company owned and operated by the Nardones.

Vince grimaced as he fought his way through the crowds to the bar. Jordan had volunteered to get this round of drinks, but Vince didn't feel right letting him do it. He was engaged to the powerful and terrifying Liesel Nardone. While she might not be as physically imposing as her brother Tommy, she was even scarier because between her and her husband to be, they could wipe a person's identity clean in minutes leaving nothing left. Yeah, better to stay in both of their good graces. And he would never have considered letting Tommy or Rex come down here from the private room they'd booked for the three-way bachelor party.

It still made Vince vaguely uncomfortable that he'd been invited to the event as a participant and not a guard.

They also had three of them stationed around the bar. They were supposed to have their own bartender in the private room, but the young man had called in sick and they were still waiting for his replacement.

Once Vince made it to the bar, the pretty woman in the tiny shorts and crop top winked at him. They already knew what he wanted, so now he just had to wait.

Out of habit, his eyes wandered, taking in the scene. Opening a nightclub had been a hit. It was the third one the Nardones owned, but the first one that had opened since they went totally legitimate. He had to admit it was working out well. Very well.

The lights down here were dim, which always made him nervous, but he ignored that and kept scanning the room. His eyes locked onto a tall redhead hurrying along the edge of the wall. She was wearing the uniform of a bartender and ducked into the back room when she reached the staff only door.

Vince's eyes narrowed. His instincts were screaming at him, but he couldn't put his finger on exactly why with her. It took another fifteen minutes before the winking bartender got him his drinks. By then Red had joined the other girls and Cici, the manager, was showing her something on the computer.

She was stunning. All long legs with creamy skin encased in thigh-high boots. Her red hair, which had been long and straight down her back, was looped up on top of her head with what looked like a pair of chopsticks.

Vince snorted and was glad no one could hear him. Red looked for all the world to be paying close attention to Cici, but Vince could tell from the tense lines of her body she was anxious about something. Was this her first night on the job? he wondered. There was no telling. He watched her the entire time he waited. Her eyes flickered around the room several times, but every time Cici showed her something, she was able to repeat it without issue.

When the tray of drinks was finally pushed his way, he put the red headed bartender out of his mind. He picked his way across the room with care and went upstairs to the private room the Nardones had reserved for themselves for this celebration.

Inside, the other four men—Rex, Tommy, Jordan, and Sawyer, one of their top lieutenants—were still playing cards.

Poker and drinks somewhere that wasn't their house or *Ciao* was what they'd finally settled on. Why they'd picked the weekend before Thanksgiving to do it, he'd never understand.

The three couples had decided back in the summer that they would do a small Christmas wedding. That had been Tommy's demand. He wanted his fiancé, Bryn, to have his name before their baby was born early in the new year.

Thankfully, none of the women had objected to something small and private. Ari had no family left other than her siblings and Bryn had only a few close people. The only hitch had been the outcry from Jordan's family that it would be small. After some frenzied back and forth, it was agreed that his nona, uncle, and aunt would attend the wedding and dinner and then their family would throw a reception after the holidays for everyone to celebrate.

Vince was happy for all three couples. Not just as his bosses, though. He, too, was a Nardone—a distant bastard cousin, but family, nonetheless. It soothed something in him to see happily ever afters for men like them.

They'd all, except Jordan, started life as ruthless mafia men. Had Tommy not found out about the existence of his, and Liesel's, much younger brother and sister, they probably would have stayed in that life. But Stella and Damien had changed the trajectory of all their lives with a healthy push from Liesel.

She'd been ready to take down the entire family until she'd seen the change in her brother and cousin.

If they could change the path of an entire family and find happiness, maybe he could find some, too. His mother had admonished him from an early age to attach himself to Tommy and rise with him. Well, he'd done so, just not in the way she'd planned.

Vince didn't know who he and his sister Heather's father was, only that he'd been a Nardone and agreed to let their mother give them the name. Sometimes Vince felt a violent rage for the man who made sure there was money in the bank, but nothing more. Those days happened less often now though, and he thought it might just be because with Tommy and Rex he had a real job and could support his mother and sister without the nameless sperm donor's child support.

---

CLARA'S HANDS shook on the doorknob to the private room. She yanked her hand back, shook it out, and stretched it out again. She breathed a sigh of relief at the steady movement. The smile pasted on her face was the one she used to rake in the big tips each night. It fooled every other man in Chicago. Hopefully, it would be enough to fool these men too.

She'd grown up in Chicago, so she knew who the Nardones were, but she'd never met them before. More than anything, she wished she wasn't right now. She didn't have any choices left, though.

Turning the knob, she threw just a tiny amount of sway into her hips as she walked into the room. Her gaze flicked to each man in turn, catching on the biggest of all of them. She stifled a gasp. It was the man whose eyes had followed her downstairs.

"Good evening, gentlemen. I'm Clara and I'll be your bartender tonight," she said, lowering her voice to the husky register she knew drove men crazy. She didn't want to lay it on too thick. Three of them were here for their bachelor party, so she didn't want to make any assumptions on how true they would be to their women.

The big one's eyes widened and then narrowed. His frank appraisal made her want to shiver, but she locked each muscle in place to prevent that from happening.

"Thank you, Clara," said one of them. She guessed it was Tommy, their leader. "Our drinks tonight are seven and seven, jack and coke, and high ball scotch on the rocks. Keep them coming please and we'll ensure you make out well tonight."

She gave a saucy toss of her head, a few strands of her hair swinging wild. "You got it, sir. I'll be right back."

Clara left the room and had to lean against the wall outside to still her shaking and slow her heart rate. She gave herself three breaths and then pushed off the wall to go down to the main bar to collect what she'd need to keep upstairs.

She hadn't been gone more than ten minutes, but she felt a noticeable shift in the mood of the room when she returned. Tuning out their conversation, she set up the tiny corner bar and then made her way to the table to see who was drinking what and if they needed a refill.

Back behind the bar, she let her glance flick over the five men. They were all big, but the giant with coal black hair and eyes drew her attention more than the others.

Taking a tray of drinks over, she bent over at all the right angles and brushed against them in the mildest suggestion. The one she assumed was Tommy gave her a knowing leer that made her stomach twist just thinking about the poor girl he was planning to make his wife.

She took the empty glasses back to the bar, emptied the ice, and cleaned them all. Her new assignment didn't change the good habits that had been drilled into her by her uncle in his bar and that had brought her such good references in the bars she'd worked at since.

It was the best legal way she knew how to make good money. Her looks, plus her skills, brought in huge tips that had only grown as she moved on to bigger and more exclusive clubs and bars.

And she needed it. Every penny she made went into paying for her father's hospital bills. He still had six months to go before he'd qualify for the medical insurance that would actually pay for something. In the meantime, his tiny pension disqualified him from many state aid programs. It was a horrific Catch-22 she'd never realized existed until her father's diagnosis of inoperable brain tumor.

Snapping fingers drew her thoughts to the men in front of her. Swallowing, she smiled.

"Did you gentlemen want some shots?" she asked.

"No," a new one spoke. "We were wondering if you'd like to make a few extra bucks tonight, Red."

Clara had to fight to keep the smile on her face. She hated that name. Like her flaming hair was her only attribute. Someday someone would take her seriously, but that day when she used her brain and not her boobs to make money was a long way off. This was exactly the opening she needed.

---

VINCE WATCHED THE RED HEAD, Clara's, face shift. It was a small change, but he noticed it and he was sure that every other man sitting around the table had as well.

Vince had spent too much of his life following his instincts. Those same gut feelings were telling him right now that this girl was trouble. The moment she'd left the room before, he'd confided his hunch to his boss, who'd just nodded and asked how he wanted to play it.

He'd run through the various options in his mind but decided drawing her out was the best way to get her to act. No one had questioned him as he laid out the plan.

Now it was time to execute it.

Clara's eyes widened eagerly. Maybe he was wrong, and she really just needed the cash, but he didn't think so. The weight of his Glock against his back was a comfort as all five men stood up. The three grooms to be lined their chairs up in the middle of the room. Sawyer fiddled with the sound system and got a thumping beat to pound out of the speakers.

"What's a bachelor party without some lap dances, eh, Red?" Rex said. Vince noted with detached interest that she didn't like that name, but she smirked and answered.

"Not much of one, that's for sure," she said, adding more sway to her walk as she strode toward them.

Each of the three men seated in the chairs looked relaxed and eager. Only someone who knew them, like Vince did, would know they were ready to react the moment something went sideways.

Clara started to dance, twirling around first, her hands touching and dragging along each man's torso. Vince had to grit his teeth as he watched, wanting to look away, but knowing he needed to be alert.

When the beat shifted, so did her movements. She bent, twisted, and shimmied around each man coming close to landing on their laps, but not quite. Vince's eyes never left her hands, though. He noticed the rest of her body and felt his own react, but he ignored it.

His cue came when her hands went to her hair as she finally straddled Tommy's lap, grinding her round ass down. He waited just one more second and was rewarded with seeing her pull one of those ridiculous hair ornaments out.

Vince had a hand on her wrists and Sawyer had his hands wrapped around her throat, forcing her to stand up. Vince shifted his grip, forcing her to drop the wicked looking stick before wrenching both arms behind her back.

He looked around, unsure what to use, but Sawyer jerked his belt out of his pants and handed it to him. With a grin, Vince took it and secured the woman's hands behind her back. She tried to stomp her foot onto his, but Rex caught her leg as she picked it up, throwing her further off balance.

"No! Stop, you don't understand," she cried. Vince wasn't moved. This woman had just tried to kill the man he respected more than any other in the world.

Jordan took a cloth napkin from the table and wound it into a rope that he forced into her mouth and secured behind her head.

"Shut up. You'll get your chance to explain eventually," Jordan said, his voice hard.

"Get her back to the house, Sawyer, and make her comfortable," Tommy ordered.

Sawyer nodded and made a quick call to the other security guards. All three entered the room and two of them lifted the woman off her feet and carried her out the door and down the stairs.

Vince watched as Tommy and Rex had a silent conversation before Tommy nodded.

"Vince," Tommy said.

"Yes, Tommy?"

"I want you to break her. Find out who and why," he said.

"You got it, boss," he said, but his stomach twisted at the idea of it. This had never been his favorite part of the job, but forcing information out of a woman made him vaguely ill.

It didn't matter, though. This was his job, and these men were his family. There was nothing he wouldn't do for them.

# TWO

Clara cried silently as two men dragged her through a side door of a huge house and down a long flight of stairs to a barren hallway. A quick glance around showed her four steel doors with keypad locks, and she flinched. She cursed herself for taking this job, but what choice had she had?

One morning, all the bills were paid. The price, kill one man. Well, she'd failed. Now, not only was her own life in danger, but her father and uncle as well.

Maybe if she just disappeared, the man would call it a wash and leave her family alone? She could only hope, especially since it was unlikely she'd leave this place alive to find out.

The two men who'd brought her here opened one of the doors and shoved her inside what was essentially a jail cell. Her hands were still bound, and her mouth gagged when the door slammed shut.

Even though she knew it wouldn't do any good, she screamed and ran to the door, pounding on it with her fists until they ached. When she finally gave up, she sank to the floor. Curling into a ball, she let the broken sobs come now.

What could she do? There was no way out of this situation. She'd failed to kill Tommy Nardone and if she told them who had sent her, then her family would pay.

She had no idea how long she lay on the floor, but eventually the sobbing stopped and so did the tears. Curveballs were too common in her life for her to fall to pieces for too long, but tonight was a doozy.

Taking a few cleansing breaths through the gag, she finally forced herself up off the floor. She scanned the room, but there was nothing helpful here. Her feet ached from the high-heeled boots, but she couldn't reach them to use the zipper. With ginger steps, she made her way across the tiny room to the cot that was bolted to the floor and the wall and lay down on it.

She shifted, trying to get comfortable. There was no way to do so with her wrists bound and still wearing leather boots, but at least she wasn't on the floor anymore. She must have dozed because she suddenly became aware of someone removing her boots and taking the belt off her wrists.

Her eyes popped open and the giant from the bar stared down at her, his face expressionless.

"Someone will bring you some water soon. I suggest you take the night to think about how you want this to go. I'll be back in the morning," he said and then he left, not waiting for her to reply.

As she lay back down, she realized he'd left a blanket on the end of the cot too. It was small and made of a rough wool yarn, but it was definitely better than sleeping in only the tiny shorts and crop top. Now that she could move her arms, she was able to get comfortable, tuck the blanket in around herself, and surprisingly, despite all that had happened that night, fall into a dreamless sleep.

# THREE

Vince watched the red-haired bartender sleep. She hadn't tried to defend herself at all up to this point. She'd cried, but otherwise said nothing. He left the nightshift security guard watching the footage with instructions to come get him if it looked like she was going to wake up and stay that way.

The bottle of water dosed with a sleeping medication was already in her cell, so hopefully she'd get a drink and go back to sleep. Once she did that, his men had instructions to put a table and an assortment of...tools in the room that he could use to interrogate her. While she slept, they were to tie her down so that she'd be completely restrained when she woke.

He went back upstairs to the office where Tommy, Rex, and Jordan were waiting.

"Did she say anything to you, or on the way over?" Rex asked.

Vince shook his head. "No, all she's done is cry."

Rex ran a hand through his hair. "It doesn't make sense. This was her first night on the job. How did she even get assigned to a private room?"

Jordan spoke up. "We have a man tailing Cici. She's the one who made the call on tonight's assignments. Liesel is deep into her financial and personal records as we speak. As the manager, she should have known better than to put a brand-new girl with a private party, so she must have been a plant.

Vince grimaced. That meant there would be one hell of a mess to clean up, and maybe in more than one place. Cici had been part of the company for the last five years as a manager at various restaurants and clubs. If she was compromised, they might have an even bigger problem.

Tommy had been staring down at his desk without saying a word through the entire exchange. He finally looked up and met Vince's eyes.

"I don't like this. This isn't how we operate anymore, and especially not with women. Do you think you can convince her you're going to hurt her without actually doing so to get what we need?"

Vince gave a mental sigh of relief, if not a physical one. At least he and Tommy were on the same page there. Rex gave them both a sharp look before nodding, and Jordan actually did let out a small sigh.

"Do we have any theories yet who might have sent her?"

Jordan shook his head. "Only guesses at this point and it's all the usual subjects—"

"But by now, none of them have both motive and means," Tommy finished. "My father would still love to take me down, but he's in an Italian prison. Rex's father is broke, but still free. Ricci has the means, but what purpose would it serve? All of our businesses are legitimate. Our will's give the remaining shares of the company to the other two cousins if something happens to one of us, and if all three of us dies, aside from a spouse benefit everything is sold and put into trust funds for Stella and Damien."

Vince nodded. "Alright, well, hopefully Red will be able to give us a few answers."

His phone buzzed with a text from the security feed monitor that the prisoner had woke up, drank the water provided, and lay back down. Perfect. She'd be out completely in less than thirty minutes. He'd go in then and strap her down, so that when she woke up she'd be totally at his mercy.

---

CLARA FELT like her body weighed three times as much as it should have as she woke up and tried to move. She was flat on her back on something hard, and it hurt. She never slept on her back because she'd hurt it when she did work as a bar back in her early twenties before she'd been promoted to bartender.

Getting her eyes open was difficult. It felt as though they were glued shut, but she managed after a few minutes of trying. She blinked a few times. Confusion set in first and then panic. The room was bare gray concrete. She was lying on...no...*strapped*, to something hard and cold.

Her breathing sped up and her eyes searched for something or someone to explain what was going on. She was supposed to be working tonight—oh, right.

She had gone to work and been sent upstairs to complete more than one assignment. And she'd failed. Oh god, they'd kill her now for sure. What would happen to her dad? Would anyone even tell him what happened to her when she didn't come home?

Tears welled hot and scared in her eyes, but she tried to

blink them away. It didn't matter what she did now, she'd die. If she held her silence, though, maybe her father would live. The man who'd come to her apartment less than twenty-four hours ago had told her so. The medical bills were paid and would continue to be paid whether she lived or died as long as she didn't tell the Nardones anything if she were to be taken.

He must have known she'd be taken. The man who'd paid her hadn't been anyone special. Average height and weight. Brown hair and eyes. Caucasian. No accent. There really wasn't anything to tell, so this shouldn't be too hard.

She wondered if it would hurt terribly. Probably. They'd probably torture her to get what she knew, but she really didn't know anything.

Minutes passed and Clara remained alone in the room. Shivers raced up and down her spine. The room was cold, the surface she laid on was cold, and she wasn't wearing much clothing.

She must have dozed off, because the next moment the giant of a man from the bar was standing beside her his golden-brown eyes boring into her green ones. His look was so intense she thought he just might be trying to see directly into her soul. For a moment, she wished he would, just to save her from what was to come, but she pushed that thought away.

This one last time she'd make a sacrifice for her father and hopefully he would live a happy, healthy life when he beat the cancer that he'd been fighting for more than five years.

More tears came, and this time she didn't try to stop them.

"Do you think crying will save you now, Red?" the giant asked, his voice absurdly soft for someone so big.

Clara gritted her teeth. She hated that nickname, but she opted for civil respect, hoping it would buy her a merciful death instead of a painful one.

"No, sir. I was just thinking about what my father will do and think when I don't return home," she told him.

"What makes you think you aren't going home?" he asked cocking his head to the side.

Clara snorted and then wished like hell she could move her hand to cover her mouth to hide that sound. "I'm sorry. It's just...well, I know who you are."

His eyes narrowed. "You know who I am?"

Clara shook her head. "Not you specifically, but who all of you are."

Now his brow furrowed. "If you know, do you want to explain why you did this? Or how you thought you'd get away with it?"

"No," she whispered.

"That's it?" he asked, incredulity thick in his voice.

"Yes," she said.

He scratched his chin thoughtfully and Clara had the most bizarre desire to lick the stubbled skin. What an absurd thought, she scolded, mentally shaking herself.

He studied her for several long minutes and then with a tiny quirk of one side of his mouth that could have been a smile, he went to the door, opened it, said something low to whoever was outside it and then came back.

Suddenly, the table she was on started to move so that she moved from lying horizontal to almost upright. The giant gave her a cold smile and stepped in close.

"I don't like to be told no, Red, so I'm going to give you one more chance to tell me what I need to know. Who sent you?"

A rush of hot and irrational anger filled her, and she

growled at him. "I hate being called that!" she shouted at him.

The quick flash of shock in his eyes gave her a momentary sense of satisfaction before he smacked her hard across the face. Her head snapped to the side and her senses reeled from that sharp sting.

Her eyes were closed as she concentrated on not crying anymore, but she became aware in the next moment that he was standing close to her. Very close. She could feel his body heat. Squeezing her eyes shut, she kept her head turned to the side.

He was having none of that though. His hand gripped her chin hard, pulling her head around so that she was facing him, but she left her eyes shut.

"Look at me, Red," he said, his voice holding a dangerous note now.

Clara grimaced, but decided she'd face this mess head on. She opened her eyes and had to stifle a gasp at how close he was. They were practically nose to nose.

"There's a good girl. Keep following directions like that and maybe I won't have to hurt you...too badly," he said with an evil grin.

Clara swallowed hard.

"Now, if you don't want me to call you Red...then why don't you tell me your real name again," he said, his voice pleasant now, as though they were strangers meeting at a party.

She inhaled sharply. Was there any harm in telling him her real name? First name, at least? She ran through it all quickly in her head and decided no, there probably wasn't.

"Clara," she finally answered.

# FOUR

*Clara.* The name settled inside Vince like a warm flame. It fit her. He was also pleased that she'd caved fairly quickly in giving him her name. He'd meant every word of what she said. If they could just get the information from her about who'd sent her, then maybe he wouldn't have to break her.

She looked stunning strapped down like that, his handprint a red blotch on her creamy skin. His dick stirred. His first reaction was disgust at himself, but then an idea occurred to him. It wasn't unexpected; his taste didn't run strictly to vanilla. Even if her's did, perhaps he could use those skills instead of typical interrogation methods to get her to give him what he wanted.

He went to the door and had a whispered conversation with the guard outside, who looked shocked, but didn't argue as he went to get the things Vince had requested. There was always a bag in his car for...emergencies.

Taking a deep breath, he turned back to his captive.

She looked scared, but determined, which in this case was terrible.

"It all boils down to one question, Clara," he said, keeping his voice even and low. "Who sent you?"

"I don't know," she said, clear and confident.

Vince frowned. He almost wanted to believe her. "Ok, we'll try one a little less clear. Why did you do it?"

This time, her lips pressed into a tight line. Ah, there it was. She might truly have no idea who'd given the orders, but her reasons for doing so were what drove her. It wasn't personal. Noted.

Vince pulled a knife from a sheath inside his jacket. Then, for effect, he shrugged it off so she could see his gun, still strapped to his side, and the rippling powerful muscles under his white dress shirt. Intimidation 101. Her eyes widened, her pretty green irises nearly obliterated in the black of her pupils.

He brought the knife to her cheek, letting her feel the wickedly sharp tip on it, before lying it flat against her skin. She wasn't even breathing now.

"Come on, Clara, help me find you a way out of this," he said and was surprised to find he meant it.

She didn't respond, although she did let her breath out in a woosh. The heat of it against his face tickled, and he had the most bizarre urge to lean in and taste her. He stepped back, resolve hardening. Sure, she was gorgeous, but that meant nothing. She'd just tried to kill one of the most important people in his life.

"Fine," he said, his voice flat now. "We'll do it your way."

He used the knife to cut away the small amount of clothing she was wearing until she was down to her underwear. He left those in place. It was part of his plan, he told himself; not a way to resist the temptation of her. No, definitely not that.

She was shaking violently already, and tears streamed down her face, but her mouth remained resolutely closed.

Vince debated for half a moment and then decided he didn't want the table for this. He reached overhead and pulled down a set of manacles on an overhead pulley system. He latched them around her wrists before unstrapping her from the table.

He should have been prepared for it, but he wasn't. So, when her foot kicked out and missed his nose by inches, crashing into his cheek instead, he was stunned for a second before he snatched the foot as it tried to connect again. He held his knife against her little toe, and she froze.

"No more of that, Clara, or we start seeing what you look like in pieces," he growled.

She let out a choked sob and went limp.

The door opened and his bag was set inside. With a sigh of relief, he went to it and pulled out a length of rope. He knelt and tied her feet to two rings in the floor. Then he walked to the door and pushed the button beside it. Her arms raised with the chains until she was up on her toes, barely able to stand.

Now he could take his time. He grabbed the bag and lowering the table back to horizontal, he lay out the contents of it on the surface.

Vince didn't watch her face, but he heard the gasps and strangled noises she let out as he put the items where she could see them. To the untrained and unknowing, they all looked like instruments of torture.

Unless you knew how much pleasure they could bring, they looked downright terrifying, which was exactly what he was going for. Vince debated for another moment and then decided to go obvious first and let the rest stew in her mind. Picking up the flogger, he let it snap out and land on her belly in a fan. She squealed and tried to curl in on herself but couldn't. He let the strokes continue to fall up and down her thighs before moving behind her. Stepping close, he whispered in her ear, "You can stop all this right now if you tell me why you did it. I believe you don't know who, but if you give me the why, I promise I can help you."

She shuddered and tried to keep herself upright, but the tears and quiet sobs were the only noises she made.

Vince gritted his teeth. He hated this. He lay down a few vicious lashes on her back that had her crying out, and then he set it to the side. Pain wasn't doing it, and he really couldn't stomach hurting her more than he was, so he changed tactics.

He ran his hands over her quivering stomach in a gentle caress. She hissed as his rough, calloused hands crossed the lash marks she already had. He grinned. His fucking dick was like iron. This was exactly how he liked his women. He shouldn't be enjoying this. It wasn't consensual and definitely didn't fall into sane or safe, but his body didn't know the difference now, did it?

In an attempt to disconcert her, he dipped one hand into the waist band of her underwear, his fingers probing her deepest center. The crisp curls...would they be red too, he wondered...hit the pads of his fingers and he continued onward and then came to an abrupt halt.

Her slick juices coated his fingers, allowing him to easily slide inside her, drawing a high-pitched whine from her.

Fuck. She was just as turned on as he was.

HEAT. It was coming from so many different directions that Clara couldn't even keep track of it anymore. So much of her skin felt tight and hot from that flogger. It felt like a sunburn without the memories of the beach. The giant's chest was pressed against her back and that felt like being laid on an exceptionally warm heating pad. But the flames? The tongues of heat licking through her body from the inside out? They were emanating from between her legs.

What. The. Fuck.

This man was hurting her. The bruising grip on her hip made that clear. And she was horny as hell.

Clara didn't have a ton of experience with sex. She'd had a few long-term boyfriends where they'd gotten to that part of the relationship. There had been moments when it felt nice, but she'd never experienced a pulsing ache of need like she did right now.

Her shame was complete when his fingers probed her center. She was soaked, her hidden folds slick with moisture. When his fingers pushed inside her, she sobbed with need and pushed her hips forward, wordlessly, and unable to help herself from begging for more.

The rough fingers caressing her silken skin froze.

"Ohhh," he said, dragging the syllable out. "You're a bad girl aren't you, Clara?" he whispered, his voice rough in her ear, ripping a shudder from her that nearly knocked her off her precarious balance on her toes.

"What?" she whimpered as his fingers began to move again. Too slowly though, just barely gliding over her flesh that now felt swollen.

"You like it when it hurts a little, don't you, Clara?" he asked.

No, she thought. Or at least, she didn't think so. That

didn't explain why she wanted more of...something right now. When she didn't answer, he stayed quiet, but continued to move his hand in a rhythmic motion she thought just might drive her crazy in another minute.

Then they were gone, and Clara let out a high-pitched whine before clamping her lips shut again. This was insane.

The giant didn't look at her as he perused the table of... implements. The giant...she couldn't keep calling him that.

"What's your name?" she asked, her voice coming out hoarse as though she'd been screaming. She thought back. Had she?

He froze and then turned to face her. "Why would I tell you that...Clara?" he asked, his voice smooth.

Something about knowing that the end was near made her feel brave for some reason. She liked this feeling. "Because I know I won't make it out of here. I want to know the name of the last person I'm going to see," she said, her voice firmer now.

"What makes you think I'm going to kill you?"

"I can't tell you what you want," she said.

The corner of his mouth quirked up in a tiny half smile. She should be scared of someone who could smile at the thought of killing her.

"My name is Vince. And I think maybe you don't want to tell me what I need to know, but you can and it's my job to make you. Killing you isn't actually helpful," he said and then paused to study her. "If you tell me why you did this, maybe I can help?"

Clara looked away and bit her lip to keep from saying anything. If she explained why she did this, he'd find her father and then he'd be in danger from two sets of people. She could not let that happen.

She just shook her head and the giant...Vince...let out a heavy breath as though he were personally disappointed by the answer.

"Hmm, we'll see," but it was a murmur as though it was only meant for him to hear.

Clara closed her eyes, which turned out to be a huge mistake. He pinched her left nipple hard enough to make her squawk with pain. Her body jerked, but that only added to the pull. His fingers didn't let up and her eyes flew open just in time to see him place the clamp. She screamed then, unable to help herself.

No amount of squirming deterred him, and the opposite side had a matching torture device clamped to it within a minute.

Then the evil man connected them with a heavy chain that swung whenever she moved and pulled on it. Her guttural cry echoed around the room as the shock of pain caused a gush of fluid between her legs. Something this awful should not be so wonderful, was all her befuddled brain could come up with.

And he wasn't done. Her eyes followed him carefully this time as he picked up a u-shaped piece of silicone. Kneeling in front of her, he peeled her boy short underwear down her hips and a flush crept up her body. He was right there. HE practically had his nose in her...oh God.

"Ungh...no, please...don't...stop..." she begged, even though that was the last thing she wanted.

"Tell me why and I'll stop," he said, his voice easy and calm.

Clara whimpered, tears welling in her eyes in frustration. "I can't...you don't understand..." she trailed off.

She gasped when he leaned in and swiped his tongue through her folds and moaned when he flicked her clit several times before pulling back. He slid the u-shaped... thing into place so that it wrapped around her pubic bone internally. Then he pulled her underwear back up and stood, moving away from her.

It didn't register that the small thing he picked up off the table next was a remote control until the *thing* whirred to life. Her body bucked, making the chain swing wildly between her nipples and she groaned, her hips jerking into the air desperate for more.

"Please...no..." she said on a ragged sob.

Her body twisted and jerked as she edged closer to release. Why was he doing this? Even though it was some sort of strange pain-pleasure, he should've stopped once he realized she wanted it.

And then it did stop. The vibration eased, and the chain was picked up, releasing the constant tension, and she cried out with the need for the sensation now.

"It's not going to be that easy...Red," he said cupping her between her legs with his big hand.

Oh. Shit.

A few seconds later, he dropped the chain and turned the toy back on. Was it more intense this time? She wasn't sure. She also wasn't sure when her eyes closed, but the feel of the flogger falling on her back felt like a loving caress now.

Until everything stopped again just as her body tensed to come.

"Nooo," she whined, forcing her eyes open to find him. "Please," she whimpered once she'd found them.

"It's not that easy, Clara. Tell me what I need to know, and I'll make it better," he coaxed.

The information was there on the tip of her tongue, but the thought of her father was sobering. It steeled her resolve...until he started again. She shrieked this time and thrashed as much as she could against the bindings, but that only made it more intense.

Her body felt tight like a rubber band pulled to its end. She was going to snap. Oh god, it was going to hurt when she came now. She didn't know how she knew that. It wasn't something she'd experienced before, but she somehow just knew it would. And it would be amazing.

But then it stopped. Again.

And she broke.

"They paid his bills," she sobbed, turning her head into her arm.

"Whose?" he demanded.

"My father's. He's sick...I tried...but I couldn't...Then they were gone. And now they'll kill him," she said, and the tears fell as her body was wracked with sobs. What kind of daughter was she, selling out her own father for an orgasm?

"Name?"

"Paul Sullivan"

"And your name?"

"Clara Sullivan," she said and forced herself to look at him. "Please," she whispered hoarsely.

But he was ignoring her. He was on his phone. He gave their names to someone on the other end.

Then he gave her what she needed. And more. The vibrator came back on, and her hands came down. The clamps came off, and she screamed as he sucked on first one and then the other leaving them aching and swollen in the sweetest way. He pushed her roughly up against the wall, yanked her underwear down, and shoved inside her with the vibrator still going.

A high, keening sound ripped from her and she shattered. Her eyes fell closed of their own volition, beautiful lights popping behind her eyelids. Awareness and consciousness faded, and the last things she noticed was the heady feel of him thrusting into her up against the wall.

Just one more thing that should be awful, but most definitely wasn't.

# FIVE

Vince stood, chest heaving as his thoughts cleared and a sense of horror dawned on him. He'd just raped a captive. His first instinct was to step away and apologize, but he realized he was holding her up. She was gone, flying high.

Dropping his head against her shoulder he let the shame of the moment wash over him. There was nothing more despicable than taking advantage of a woman with no power.

A small voice in the back of his mind insisted it was fine since she *obviously* enjoyed it, but he ignored that.

Taking several long breaths he forced his thoughts to move in a coherent direction, which was hard since he was still pressed up against her. His first thought was he needed to get her out of this cell.

He pulled his phone out of his pocket and dialed.

"Vince?" Tommy asked, the question evident in his voice.

"I need a blanket and room that I can shut her in," he said trying to keep his voice brusque, but his voice broke just a little on the word "her."

There was a long beat of silence on the other end of the line, but when it answered, "Alright," Vince let out a sigh of relief.

"Did Liesel find anything?"

That got a quiet chuckle. "Of course. We've already sent an extraction team. What do we do with her?"

This time it was Vince who was quiet. "Whatever you think is best, boss," he said, trying to mean it.

"Mmm, well tonight's not the time to think about it. We'll discuss it tomorrow and make a decision. You're responsible for her until then."

Vince swallowed hard. "Of course," he answered.

"Get some sleep. I'll find you in the morning," Tommy said and then the line went dead.

A moment later, there was a quiet knock on the door. Vince gathered Clara in his arms and placed her on the table. She whimpered and curled into a ball. Was she scared or cold from being away from him?

Opening the door he took the blanket and the key for a room on the second floor of the house. It had been designed for multiple families to live together including several two-room suites that locked both inside and out.

He wrapped Clara in the blanket and followed the man outside the door up the two flights of stairs. He stayed only long enough to set the key on the bedside table in the first of the two bedrooms and then left, closing the door with a quiet click.

Vince stood, hesitant for a moment. Should he put her in her own room and lock her in or put her in bed here and sleep next to her? She was still a prisoner. He really shouldn't stay close in case she woke up and tried something. On the other hand, he really didn't like the idea of leaving a masochist alone after they hit subspace. Especially since, if he had to guess, she hadn't even known she was a masochist before tonight.

In the end, he decided that he'd tie her hands loosely and put her in bed with him. Only to be close by for when she came down. Not because she was a nearly irresistible combination for him. He was much more professional than that.

It didn't make any difference that she was an attractive woman, he told himself. All while knowing it was a complete lie.

Before he could lie down with her though he had to check in with Tommy and Rex before going to sleep. He knocked on the office door and they bade him enter.

"What's the story?" he asked once the door was shut.

Rex looked up from his seat around the conference table. "Her father has cancer. They're both thousands in debt. Or at least they were."

Vince winced.

Tommy rubbed a hand over his face.

"Who paid her?" Vince asked.

"Liesel's still working on that, but we moved her father to one of the secure private rooms at the hospital on the same floor as Damien so our guys can keep an eye on him. We're making arrangements to move them both here tomorrow with our private doctors and nurses. They'll consult with the hospital staff as needed."

"How is she?" Rex asked, his eyes telling Vince Rex understood how much he disliked hurting women...unless they wanted to be hurt that is.

"She's fine. It didn't take much to make her talk," he answered.

Rex nodded. "That's good."

Vince waited, but when neither man said anything he asked, "What are we going to do with her?"

The two men exchanged a look. "For now she stays our prisoner. I don't think it was personal, but we need to know who paid her. Once we do, they we can decide how much danger she's in or if she's too much of a liability," Tommy said.

Vince managed to keep his face neutral this time.

"Until we know, you're in charge of her. Let us know if you need a break and we'll arrange something, but with the wedding coming up—"

"I know, you're all busy," Vince said with a smile. He was so happy for his cousins. They were all distant family, and while he wasn't a real Nardone, the two men in front of him never treated him as less because of it. "I got it. Can she leave the rooms, or do you want me to keep her completely contained?"

Rex and Tommy exchanged another look. "As long as you're with her she's free to go anywhere in the house."

"Alright. Goodnight, boss," Vince said and let himself out of the office as the two men returned it.

Back upstairs, he stared down at Clara and her fiery mane of hair spread out over the pillow. She was still out, thank goodness. He stripped off his shoes and socks and lay down close by, but not touching her. He still felt guilty about using her like that, but her response had been so fucking beautiful that it had overwhelmed him. It didn't excuse his behavior though, and he knew it.

As he settled against the pillow, the bed shifted and she rolled into him, lying her head on his shoulder, her bound hands resting on his chest. Warmth suffused him. It probably didn't mean anything, but even in her sleep she turned toward him.

Hopefully, that meant she wouldn't hate him in the morning.

# SIX

Clara ached all over. What the hell had she done last night at work that left her feeling like this? She rolled over and her hands wouldn't come apart. Her eyes flew open, and she came face to face with the giant from last night. He was dressed, but she wasn't.

The memories from the night before slammed into her and she gasped. The giant...Vince was his name she remembered...jerked awake. His eyes flitted around the room as though searching for the threat before coming to rest on her.

"Are you alright?" he asked his voice rough with sleep.

She opened her mouth, shut it, and then opened it again. "I'm tied up and naked. Do you think I'm alright?" she snapped.

It took several seconds after the words spilled out to realize that antagonizing this man probably wasn't the best choice.

"I'm sorry—"

"Don't be," he said with a tiny half smile. "You're right. I'll ask the girls if any of them have something you can wear.

Bryn is shorter than you, but otherwise your build is about the same."

Girls? There were other women around? She didn't get a chance to ask because Vince had rolled from the bed. Without looking at her, he moved toward the door. He paused when he opened it, but still didn't look at her.

"The bathroom is through there," he said gesturing toward an open door. "I'll be back as soon as I can with some clothes and food."

Then he left without giving her a chance to answer.

She waited several minutes, but when it seemed he really was leaving her alone, she eased out of the bed. She couldn't help but groan at the soreness of her muscles and skin. She felt like she had a sunburn. In the bathroom she looked at her back in the mirror and grimaced. She looked like she had one too. Her skin was pink with a faint shine to it where the marks crisscrossed her body.

She used the bathroom and cleaned up as much as she could with her hands tied in front of her and then crawled back in the bed. For those few moments she'd been able to keep the thoughts of the previous night in the back of her mind, but now they rushed back, and she was forced to confront them. She'd essentially signed her father's death warrant, and that thought broke her heart. She'd been doing everything she could for the last several years to help him get through his battle with cancer.

She hadn't asked for the help the stranger had given her, but he'd made it clear that it needed to be repaid how he asked or both she and her father would suffer. If she was honest, there had never been a real chance of her succeeding. Murder was the price.

Clara was a vegetarian because even the idea of killing animals made her ill. Tears formed in her eyes and spilled down her cheeks. Now her father was probably already dead. Not that she was in any better position. She was tied up naked in the bed of the man who had tortured her confession out of her.

Maybe it was a good sign that he was going to feed and clothe her. He probably wasn't planning to kill her if he was going to that trouble, right? What kind of life could she have to look forward to though? If Vince didn't kill her, the man who had paid her probably would.

Her stomach twisted painfully.

There was a knock on the door. She didn't think about it, but when the knock came again, she realized whoever it was didn't plan to come into the room unless she answered.

"Come in," she said.

The door opened revealing a tall blonde woman sporting a moderately sized baby bump.

"Good morning," the woman said with a small smile that didn't quite reach her eyes.

"Good morning," Clara answered. What did this woman think about her being here naked with her hands tied?

"I brought you some clothes. I've also got permission to untie your hands so you can shower, as long as I warn you that I'm a former cop and I can incapacitate you without much effort. And my fiancé will not be happy if you try anything stupid. There's no way out of this house unless one of us takes you."

The woman said all this with a very matter-of-fact air that terrified Clara.

"I promise I won't do anything," Clara said, keeping her eyes down.

"Good," the woman said her voice a lot warmer now.

"I'm Bryn, by the way. The man you tried to kill last night is my fiancé."

Clara's eyes flew up, and she opened her mouth to say she was sorry, but then the woman, Bryn, started laughing.

"Don't worry about it. There are still some days I want to kill him too, but I am glad you didn't succeed."

Clara tried to come up with some way to reply to this that made sense, but nothing came to mind, so she just nodded.

Bryn stepped in close and tugged the rope loose from her wrists. Clara rubbed the places the rope had been, but there weren't any visible marks.

"Go get cleaned up. I'll wait here," Bryn said, settling onto a small settee that was situated along one wall.

Clara hesitated for just a moment. She was still naked. Bryn was ignoring her, or at least she seemed like it. Clara had a feeling that she was observing her every move but was trying not to make things awkward.

In the bathroom she turned the water on as hot as she could stand. She hissed when it hit her skin, but she needed it. In her mind the water was washing away more than just dirt and sweat. It took all her fear and worry with it. She'd learned this trick on a podcast and it was one of the few things that had helped her deal with the stress of the last few years. The water took it all away, and she was able to look at whatever situation she was facing with new eyes.

She had to admit though, this was unlike any obstacle she'd faced before.

---

VINCE KNOCKED on the door before going in. Bryn was in there while Clara had some time to clean up and get dressed. He was honestly amazed he'd slept at all last night. Lying in bed and having her curled up around him had been nothing short of torture.

He already fucked up, literally, once; he was not going to do it again. He confessed what happened to Tommy and Rex this morning. Surprisingly, they'd just exchanged a look and told him they expected better going forward.

Vince shrugged, his shirt suddenly feeling too tight. This new way of dealing with things was going to take some getting used to. Of course, the previous leadership probably would have encouraged what he did rather than punishment.

"Come in," he heard Bryn call from the other side of the door. He opened it but kept his eyes down. He placed the tray of eggs, toast, and fruit on the small table.

"She's still drying her hair," Bryn said unnecessarily, since he could hear the hair dryer running in the bathroom.

"How is she?"

Bryn shrugged. "Good, I guess. She hasn't said much."

"Did you tell her who you were?"

"Of course," Bryn said. "But I also told her that I don't hold it against her. Some days I want to kill him too," she finished with a grin.

Vince couldn't help his answering smile. This woman was absolutely perfect for Tommy. Even if they had still been in the old business, Bryn was the type of woman who could stand beside Tommy and lead, not a vapid *principessa* or a bimbo like Arturo Nardone's second wife.

"I'm heading down to the library. Liesel, Ari, and I have a meeting to finish up the wedding details." She paused and looked toward the door. "You can bring her down when she's done if you have things you need to get done," she added.

He didn't have anything to do, but it was probably for the best that he not spend much time with Clara. "Alright, I will, thanks."

Bryn looked at the closed door, her face pensive. "What are you guys going to do with her?"

Vince sucked in a sharp breath. There was a perfect example. Bryn knew there was no way they could just send Clara on her way. She knew too much about them and was in danger of being targeted the moment she stepped outside the house by whoever had sent her once they knew she failed.

"Tommy said she stays for now. Jordan is still working on figuring out who sent her."

Bryn nodded with a small frown. "I don't like the idea of keeping her prisoner, but she isn't safe outside of here."

Tommy had just said as much to him not ten minutes ago.

"Oh well, we'll figure it out as we go, I guess. It's what we always do, anyway," she said with a small smile. "I'll see you downstairs in a bit."

Vince nodded and took the seat she'd just left to wait for Clara to finish up. He tried not to stare at the door he knew she'd have to come through, but he couldn't keep his eyes away. So, when she stepped out he was watching. Her red hair hung in a floating cloud around her head and ended at the bottom of her ribs. She was wearing leggings that came to mid-calf with a purple tunic.

Vince swallowed hard. He didn't think he'd ever seen a more beautiful woman, but wisely kept that thought to himself.

"Are you ready?" he asked, his voice rougher than usual.

She started. Apparently she hadn't realized he was there. "For what?" she squeaked.

"You're going downstairs to the library with Bryn and the girls for the morning. I have some things to take care of. You can eat first, though," he said, gesturing toward the table.

Her eyes darted back and forth from him to the food and back again. "It's safe," he assured her, trying not to be irritated by the fear in her eyes.

She froze, her eyes locked on him. "I know," she said, her voice soft now. "I was just surprised. How did you know I don't eat meat?"

Vince shrugged. "I didn't. I just asked them to put together something simple for you. I didn't know if you were allergic to eggs, though. If you are, I can have some oatmeal brought up."

She shook her head. "I'm not," she said, pausing before continuing. "Thank you...Vince," she finished.

Vince forced himself not to react to the sound of his name on her lips. "You're welcome. Eat up," he said and pulled out his phone to give himself something to do. He usually left his phone alone ninety percent of the time, but he needed something to keep himself from staring at her as she ate. He kept his eyes glued to the screen, so he didn't see her finish and come over to him until she sat down next to him.

He started, but she just looked at the floor.

"What happens to me now?" she asked.

Vince swallowed hard. "For now, you stay here as a guest of the Nardone family."

"Guest?"

"It sounds better than being under house arrest. As long as you're with me, one of the other guys, Bryn, or Liesel, you're free to roam the house."

"I know why Bryn, but who is Liesel?"

Vince smiled. "You'll meet her in a few minutes, but I'll warn you now not to underestimate her. She's probably the most dangerous one of all of us. I've seen her shoot a man in the knee and hack a national security system in the same half hour time span."

Clara's mouth fell open, and she was staring at him now. Apparently she decided not to pack that comment. "But what *happens* to me?"

"Nothing really. We can't let you go until we know who sent you and eliminate them."

That got her attention. "What?"

"This wasn't your plan was it?" he asked.

She shook her head.

"Well, then, when whoever paid your father's bills figures out you failed, they'll come after you to clean up their mess. We don't know who it was yet, but Jordan is working on it."

She wrinkled her nose. "Who's Jordan?"

"The only one that's close in size to me and almost as dangerous as Liesel with a computer."

She nodded, her face thoughtful and then it twisted into a grimace. "What about my father?"

"Safe," Vince said, but that was all he could tell her for now on Tommy's orders.

"What does that mean?"

Vince sighed. "I can't explain that right now. You'll just have to trust me."

He braced for her fury. What cause did she have to trust him after all? He'd tortured her and then raped her last night. Maybe she didn't remember the second part, but she damn well would the first.

"Alright," she finally said, and Vince's head snapped up to look at her.

She gave him a wry smile. "What, you expected me to argue with you?"

Vince just shrugged, not sure how to answer that.

"I do trust you. I know you could have actually hurt me last night, or killed me for that matter, but you didn't," she said and to Vince's amazement she was blushing. His heart stuttered and then sped up. It had seemed like she was enjoying herself at the time, but he still felt guilty.

"Good. Hopefully, we'll have news soon. For now, though, it's time to head downstairs."

"What are they doing down there?" she asked.

Now he really smiled. "Wedding planning," he said and reveled just a little in the look of absolute shock on her face.

# SEVEN

Vince accompanied her down two flights of stairs and showed her to a large bright room. Every wall was built-in shelves full of books. There were two overstuffed leather couches and a huge wooden desk at opposite ends of the room.

The woman she'd already met, Bryn, was seated with her feet propped up on a table between the couches. Two other women sat with her. One with brown hair piled on top of her head and the other with blue-black hair. That last one had a notebook balanced on her lap.

"So for flowers we decided red and white roses in small bouquets for each of us and red for the guys right?"

"I thought we were getting white lilies?" the brown-haired one ask.

"We can't, they made Bryn sick when she smelled them."

Vince cleared his throat and all three women looked up at him.

"Ladies, this is Clara," he said.

Bryn gave her a small smile, but the other two just

stared. "Clara, this is Liesel. She's Tommy's sister," Bryn said pointing at the woman with brown hair.

"And I'm Ari, I'm engaged to Rex," the one with black hair said introducing herself.

"I'll be back to get her when I'm done," Vince said, and Clara tried not to wince at the idea she needed to be watched constantly. She knew no amount of assurance from her would make them understand she wasn't a danger to them. They'd see eventually.

"No problem. We've still got a lot to do here and then we'll go up for lunch," Liesel said eyeing her with interest. Vince backed from the room leaving her alone with them. Bryn patted the couch beside her.

"Come on, have a seat. We don't bite. Well, Liesel might, but probably not," Bryn said with a smirk.

Liesel threw a crumpled piece of paper at her. "I do not bite," she hissed.

"Oh yeah, what was that on Jordan's neck last week then?"

Liesel blushed but didn't back down. "That was a hickey, which is sucking. Don't you know the difference, Ari? You show up often enough with them."

"I know sometimes teeth are involved," Ari retorted

Clara couldn't help but stare, mouth agape at the three of them discussing sex. She felt her face heat as they talked.

"Alright, back to business you two. We have a lot to go over and you're embarrassing Clara," Bryn said.

Ari and Liesel gave each other a look before returning to their list.

"Ok, so roses. Betsy is handling the food and won't let us anywhere near it. The minister agreed to come to the house even though he was a little confused by the whole three weddings on Christmas Eve thing.

"You guys are getting married Christmas Eve?" Clara blurted out.

All three girls turned to stare at her, but it was Liesel who answered. "Yes, is that a problem?"

Clara lowered her eyes. "Sorry, no. I think that's awesome. If I ever got married, I always wanted a holiday wedding."

Liesel gave her a hard look before nodding. "Yes, Tommy wanted Bryn to have his last name before junior—"

"Or juniorette," Ari cut in.

Liesel raised one eyebrow at her. "Makes their appearance."

Clara wanted to ask Bryn about the baby but decided she should probably just keep her mouth shut.

"Did the guys get their suits yet?" Ari asked.

"They had the fitting last week," Liesel said.

"Bryn, when do you think you want to schedule your final dress fitting? Liesel and I already went, but with you..." she trailed off.

"I'll go the second week of December. Liz said she could make that work," Bryn answered.

Ari made a note on the paper.

"What about the clothes for the kids?" Bryn asked.

"Damien and Owen will go with the guys to get their suits when they pick up theirs. Stella and Olivia go tomorrow to try their dresses on," Ari answered.

"They're wearing the green right?"

"Yup," said Ari, then she sighed. "Alright, last thing, guest list."

"We're not inviting anyone except Vince and Sawyer," Liesel said. "The rest of our family doesn't deserve the name and we don't want to invite all our employees. Sawyer is like family," she finished.

Bryn nodded. "My brother, my mom, and Sophie. That's it for me," she said.

Ari wrote all that out. "I don't have anyone either. What about Jordan?" she asked Liesel.

She grimaced. "Yeah, his family isn't happy, but we're still working on it," she said. "I'll get him to short list it soon, but he's been busy the last two days," she continued with a sidelong glance at Clara.

She didn't know what to say. Was it appropriate to apologize in this kind of situation? In the end, Clara decided staying quiet was probably for the best.

"Leave her alone, Liesel," Bryn said, her voice firm.

"What? I think she's brave. Not many people have the guts to look Tommy in the eye, let alone try to kill him with a hair accessory."

Clara let out her breath in a woosh. She wanted to run from the room rather than continue to face these three. That wasn't an option, though. Vince had made that clear. Did they already know why she'd done it and just wanted to torture her?

"I said leave her be. We've all had to make hard decisions this year. She's no different," Bryn said her voice icy now.

"You're right, Bryn," Ari said.

Liesel stuck her tongue out at the two of them, instantly lightening the mood, and all three women laughed.

None of them noticed the door opening until Vince spoke. "Clara, can you come with me please? Liesel, Damien is in his room. He wants to see you," he said.

Liesel jumped up and bolted out the door without hesitation.

Ari rolled her eyes. "I guess we're done here. I'll see you later, Clara. She's coming to dinner, right Vince?"

"That's not up to me, Ari," he said.

"Then I insist," she said.

Clara wanted to tell her not to worry about it. She didn't want to be the cause of any discord here.

Vince just smiled though. "Then I guess she'll be there. We should go for now, Clara," he insisted.

She got up and followed him. He led her back up the two flights of stairs and she thought they were going back to the room they'd slept in, but he kept going past that room.

He pushed open the door and gestured for her to go first. She stepped inside and stopped short. Her father was lying in a hospital bed, hooked up to several machines. There was a young nurse checking the monitors who looked up and smiled when she saw her.

"You must be Clara," she said. "I'm Cady."

"Nice to meet you," she said automatically, but her eyes were only for her father. Who was alive. Here.

She turned to look at Vince and he gave her a small smile. She couldn't help it. She threw herself into his arms, hugging him tight. "Thank you," she whispered, and kissed his cheek.

---

VINCE STOOD FROZEN EVEN after Clara pulled away and sat at her father's side. Her arms...that kiss, it felt too good.

He'd spent the last hour getting everything ready for her father and Damien. He knew she would be glad he was safe, but she would have questions he couldn't answer. She didn't ask though. Didn't even look at him when her father started asking questions.

"What's going on, Clara?" he asked her, his voice weak.

She squeezed his hand and, while he couldn't see her face, he imagined she was distressed by this. "I don't really know, Dad. Some things...happened. I really can't explain, but I'm so glad you're here."

"Where is here?"

He watched her red hair shimmer as she shook her head. "Dad, please..." she begged, trailing off.

"I told you not to worry about the bills, honey," he said, and Vince heard him trying to force some steel into his voice, though it fell short.

"I know and I wasn't, but..." she stopped and turned to look at him.

Warmth bloomed in his chest that she'd turned to him for help, even if it was only in this.

"You and your daughter will be safe here, Mr. Sullivan, and you'll get the care and treatment you need," Vince assured them both.

Clara's father narrowed his eyes and studied Vince. "Why?"

Vince shrugged. "It's just the way it has to be," he said, his voice leaving no room for argument.

"How did you meet my daughter?"

"She was the bartender at my cousin's bachelor party," he said.

"And you immediately moved her in with you?" he asked, skepticism lacing his voice.

Clara spoke up, surprising them both. "Sometimes you just know," she said. "I know what you meant about Mom now," she finished.

She wasn't looking at her father now. Her eyes were fixed on Vince, pleading with him to go along with it. He swallowed hard. That was a little too close to the truth for him. She was gorgeous, caring, and needed the pain he loved to give, but he knew what she was asking.

If her father thought they were in love, it made all of this a little easier to explain.

Her father's eyes widened. "You're in love with him, Clarbear?"

He saw her wince at the childish nickname, but Vince kind of loved it.

She was looking at him when she answered though. "From the moment I laid eyes on him."

Vince stiffened, but Clara was looking back at her father. They were talking now about his treatment plan and what was going to change now that he'd be receiving private care.

"You must be made of money, to afford all this," Mr. Sullivan said. It took Vince a moment to realize he was talking to him.

"Not me. My cousins are though," he assured him.

He read the disbelief in the man's face, but there was no other explanation to be given for now.

There was a long pause and then he heard him say in a low whisper, "Clara, you don't have to do this," he hissed.

"Do what?"

Another pause, then, "Give yourself to them for me. I've fought hard, but I don't think I'm going to win this one."

He heard Clara's sharp inhale. "Dad, I—"

Vince stepped in. "Mr. Sullivan, I love your daughter. My family takes care of its own and you're a part of that now."

The man looked him up and down, then finally nodded. "I see," he said and turned back to Clara who was staring up at Vince with a look in her eyes he couldn't read.

"Well, I'm here now, Clarbear, but I'm exhausted. You'll come back later?"

"Of course," she said.

Her father closed his eyes and Clara sat by his side holding his hand for another minute. With a quick squeeze she stood, leaned in, and kissed his forehead, and came over to Vince where he stood by the door.

He opened the door, letting her go out first. Outside in the hall, she sagged against the wall. Finally, she raised her eyes to his. "Thank you," she whispered, but it sounded choked as though she was trying not to cry. "I know you didn't have to do that—" she said, but her voice cracked, and a tear leaked out of the corner of her eye.

Vince didn't think, he reached for her and pulled her into his chest. She melted into his embrace. This wasn't the place for her to breakdown though. Sweeping her up in his arms, he carried her back to the suite they were sharing. Once inside, he settled onto the bed with her and simply held her.

The last forty-eight hours had to have been hell for her. When you weren't used to this life, a crash course in it was a lot to handle. He didn't try to stop her from crying, just rubbed her back in soothing circles and pressed his lips to her hair. The words he whispered didn't make sense, but he said them anyway.

He was so wrapped up in the feeling of her so close to him, that he completely missed her going still and her breathing going soft and rhythmic. She was asleep in his arms.

This felt good. Too good.

# EIGHT

She was dreaming. She must be. The sense of peace that she felt in her bones right now wasn't something she'd felt in a long time. Awareness returned slowly, but when it hit her that she was wrapped in strong arms and pulled against a broad, firm chest she jerked awake.

The arms let go of her immediately.

Clara's eyes snapped open, and she found herself looking into the guarded eyes of Vince. Her tormentor and her savior.

"Are you alright?" he asked, his voice soft.

"Yes," she said, but it came out as a croak. She cleared her throat. "Yes, I'm fine. Thank you."

He frowned. "For what?"

"For telling my father that we were..." she trailed off and felt heat creeping up her neck into her cheeks. It was embarrassing now that her father thought she'd whored herself out to get him care. It was so much worse. There was no telling how long he'd be around, but it was definitely better that he not believe she was capable of attempted murder. She grimaced.

"I'm sorry," he said, and her eyes snapped to his.

"You have nothing to be sorry for," she said, her voice barely above a whisper.

He grimaced. "I have many things to be sorry for, but that was presumptuous. We'll come up with something to tell him later."

She looked away. Oh, of course. He wouldn't want to pretend to be in love with her indefinitely. She'd tried to kill his family.

"It's ok," she blurted out.

His brow furrowed. "What is?"

"Um, telling him that as long as you don't mind," she said not meeting his eyes now. "I mean, I know you don't, and so does your family. You can't—"

"Why not?"

She stopped, stunned by that. "What?"

"Why can't I?"

"Because I tried to kill your cousin. He'll find out it's a lie," she said. Where was he going with this?

To her surprise he laughed. "Did the girls tell you how they got together with their men?"

Clara shook her head, mystified.

"Attempted murder really wouldn't be the strangest reason two people got together in this house," he assured her. Then he sobered. "I get it though. I won't say it again. I don't want to make you uncomfortable," he said, and she heard the sober promise in his voice. "If I do, I need you to tell me. I'm sure you don't trust me, but I promise not to hurt you again."

She gaped at him. Her brain tried to process the upside-down nature of what he was saying. He didn't want her to be uncomfortable? He was worried about her lack of trust, when he'd done everything he could to keep her safe and get her father to her.

Then it dawned on her. He meant last night when they'd...oh.

"I do," she blurted out.

"You do what?" he asked cautiously.

"Trust you."

His eyebrows flew up. "You do? Why?"

"You could have hurt me last night—"

"I did hurt you," he interrupted.

"Well yeah, but you could have really hurt me," she said confused. "My dad is safe and so am I...unless your cousin has something else planned for me?" she finished, the question in her voice making it tremble.

Vince shook his head slowly. "No, he knows you were doing what you had to do to protect your family. Tommy understands and respects that. Aren't you angry about what happened last night?"

She cocked her head to the side. "Why would I be? I deserved much worse. You guys could have me in prison right now and then my father would be dead," she shook her head, the truth dawning on her. She really was safe. Maybe eventually she could get back to her life. In the meantime though...

Without letting herself think about it too much she swung her leg over Vince's outstretched legs, so she was straddling his lap. He let out a surprised grunt and gave her a wary look.

"What are you doing, Clara?"

"Honestly? I'm not sure," she said. And she meant it. But she knew she wanted this, so without giving him a chance to respond, she leaned in and kissed him hard.

VINCE SAT FROZEN. The shock of her lips on his held in him in thrall until her tongue licked his bottom lip He grabbed her shoulders and pushed her back.

"Clara, stop," he said, his voice harsh.

Her eyes widened. Her body went stiff, and she tried to scramble away, but Vince's grip didn't let up. She started to struggle, and Vince rolled them so he could use his weight to pin her down.

"Clara, stop," he demanded again and grabbed her head between his hands to force her to look at him.

She went still.

Tears shimmered in her eyes, and he wanted so badly to kiss her and make it better, but that wouldn't be right.

"I'm sorry," she whispered.

"You don't need to be sorry," he said back, his voice soft now. "I'm not angry with you. No one is. We know what it means to do anything for the people you love."

"I meant I'm sorry for throwing myself at you. I'm sure—"

"I have never wanted a woman the way I want you, sweetheart, but it wouldn't be right."

Her brow furrowed. "Why?"

Vince wanted to look away. It still shamed him the way he'd taken her like that.

"I took everything from you without consent. Don't get me wrong, I like it rough—"

"I could tell," she said with a cheeky smirk, and Vince couldn't help his answering smile.

"But I have never raped anyone before," he admitted his stomach twisting in revulsion.

She reached up and caressed his face with gentle

fingers. "That wasn't rape, Vince. I begged you for it," she said her voice stronger now.

"It might as well have been," he said turning his head to kiss her palm, unable to help himself.

Now it was her who turned his head back to look at her. "Vince, you could have tortured, maimed, and killed me. You didn't. Instead, you drove me to unbelievable heights of pleasure that I didn't even know existed. And you saved my father. I understand if you don't want me, but make no mistake, I want you."

Vince searched her face and found only truth there.

He leaned down and pressed a soft kiss to her lips. They were so soft under his. All he did was kiss her for long minutes, and when he finally delved into her mouth with his tongue he groaned at the exquisite taste of her.

She clung to him. He gave into it then. He wouldn't think about it beyond this moment, and when she eventually came to her senses he'd step back, but for now he wasn't strong enough to resist.

He rolled onto his back, taking her with him. Loosening his grip he let her take over. She'd been the one to start it, let her take it where she would. He'd gladly go along for the ride.

# NINE

"Clara," he whispered against her hair.

In answer, she snuggled closer to him.

"Sweetheart, I know you're sleepy, but I need you to pay attention," he said laughter filling his voice. Just being near her made him feel lighter, but this? Holding her... loving her...it was everything he never knew had been missing. Could she possibly feel the same way?

She harrumphed and opened her eyes, the green pools hazy still.

"I have to tell Tommy what's going on," he said when he was sure she was really paying attention. Her eyes narrowed. If she hadn't been before, she definitely was now.

"Why?"

Vince sighed and hugged her to him. "Whether you did it on your own or not, you tried to kill him two days ago. He's my boss, but more importantly he's my family. I can't hide this from him."

"Aren't you a grown-up who makes your own decisions?" she snarked.

He laid a series of five hard swats on her ass that had her shrieking and trying to roll from his arms.

"Don't be a brat, Clara. This is the right thing to do, and you know it."

Her cheeks were stained pink with outrage, and she glared at him for a long minute. When she spoke though, it was soft and laced with fear. "What if he says no?"

Vince's eyes softened. "He won't if we're honest with him. Tommy is a fair man, but I can't go behind his back. I trust him with my life, and he trusts me with his. But..." he hesitated, and she looked back at him.

"But what?"

"Whether we do this or not, you know you can't leave here, right?"

She frowned. "Ever?"

"No, not forever, but it'll be awhile. At least until we find—" He was interrupted by the ringing of his cell phone.

Without hesitation he answered. Even lying naked next to his lover he wasn't going to ignore a call from Tommy.

"Jordan found them...him," Tommy said.

"Who?"

"Roman and Enea...they were trying to kill me to get money to bail out Arturo. I guess he never explained what was happening to them."

"So what now?"

"Liesel and Jordan are drying up the rest of their funds. They'll be on their own stuck in Italy within twenty-four hours."

"What's next?" he asked, needing to know what would happen to Clara and her father.

"I need to talk to your girl," Tommy said.

"She's not—"

"Vince," Tommy commanded.

"Yes, boss?"

"Stop talking so I don't have to beat you down for lying to me. You will both come to family dinner tonight and the three of us will meet immediately afterward."

He glanced down at Clara who was watching him.

"Of course," he murmured.

"Good man, six sharp. Take that girl shopping and get her some clothing that fits."

"Will do, boss."

He hung up and stared up at the ceiling. He wondered if the elder Nardones would ever learn their lesson. They'd stepped away, and now that they were unhappy with the direction of things, they thought they could force things to change.

"What happened?"

"It was Tommy's uncle and stepmother who paid the money for your dad to make you help them. They've wanted Tommy dead for several months now since they realized they can't reason with him."

She swallowed hard. "So what will happen to my dad and I now?"

Vince saw the fear etched in her face. He didn't have an answer right now because it wasn't his decision to make. "We'll find out after dinner. It can't be too bad though, Tommy wants me to take you shopping for some clothes that fit you."

"I have clothes at home," she said.

Vince shrugged. "I have my orders," he said with a smirk. As though he needed convincing to spoil this woman. In his mind, she deserved it. It seemed as though she'd been fighting battles on her own for a long time.

If things went well, would he be able to stand beside her for them in the future? Would Tommy let him? Would she?

---

THE RIDE to the boutique didn't take long. Vince maneuvered the massive black SUV through the tight streets of a small neighborhood with ease, even down to the parallel parking job directly in front of the store.

He was out of the car and around to her before she'd finished unbuckling her seatbelt. His hand swallowed her's as he helped her down and a tiny shiver raced over her skin at the delicious feeling of being cared for. It was an unusual one for her and all the more powerful for it.

His hand moved to the small of her back, guiding her across the sidewalk. She looked at the sign overhead for *Bellissima* and grimaced. She loved pretty clothes as much as the next girl, but it had been years since she'd shopped anywhere but a clearance rack. Everything she had went into the basics for her and anything left went to her father. He might rage that she shouldn't be taking care of him, but he was all she had left.

The pressure of Vince's hand and a quick glance to her right made that thought pause. Maybe that wasn't true anymore.

Inside a petite woman who barely came up to her shoulders rushed forward.

"Vince," she said gliding toward them on sky high heels.

"Liz," he greeted her with a warm embrace and a kiss on the cheek that had irritation roiling in her stomach. Clara clamped her teeth shut to avoid saying anything. It didn't matter.

He turned back to her and thankfully didn't seem to notice her internal discord. "This is Clara. She's a guest of the family. She had to come stay with us unexpectedly and I want to get her some new clothes while she's here. Clara, this is Liz, Jordan's sister. She owns this place," he said giving Liz an affectionate smile that made her want to claw the woman.

She froze, then forced a smile to her lips. It must not have been completely convincing because Vince frowned at her. Clara cleared her throat.

"It's nice to meet you, Liz. I'd appreciate any help you can give me. I can pay for my own clothes," she said with her own frown back at him.

"We'll just a look around for a minute, Liz, and then I'll leave you ladies to it," he said his hand gripping her wrist and tugging her toward the changing room.

Once inside he pinned her up against the wall with his body and kissed her hard.

"I like that you're jealous, sweetheart, but forget about it. Liz is like a sister to me. I've known her family since her parents died and she and Jordan came to live with their uncle and nona. That's just how we say hello," he assured her.

Clara glared at him. "That's an awfully friendly hello, and I'm not jealous," she hissed.

His hand snaked into her hair, pulling her head back. He very deliberately sank his teeth into her jaw until she squeaked, then kissed her again, his tongue forcing its way inside her mouth and dueling with hers until she moaned and melted against him.

He pulled back and gave her a wolfish smile. "See the difference, sweetheart?" he asked his low voice rumbling right through his chest into her's.

Clara nodded against the hold he had on her hair. "Good girl, now behave and listen to Liz. She knows what she's doing. I'll be waiting in the car," he said.

Clara watched Liz flit around on her heels after Vince

left. She gathered dresses, slacks, jeans, sweaters. And even shoes. She tried on piece after piece, Liz giving kind, but useful feedback.

Clara blushed the first few times she barged into the dressing room while she was down to her underwear. Liz just tutted and brought back an arm full of lingerie.

She tried to protest that she was only there for one outfit, but Liz just waved her off with, "These are Tommy's orders."

What kind of weird backward world was she living in that the man she'd tried to kill was buying her new clothes?

Clara admired the lavender lace bra and panties and then saw the price tag. She swallowed hard and put it down. Holy shit what kind of money were these people made of?

Liz was back a moment later and saw the discarded lace. "Don't you like the color? I think it's perfect."

"It's too much," she said not meeting the other woman's eyes.

When Liz laughed, she snapped her head up. "Do you have any idea who these men are?"

Clara gave her a blank look. Who didn't know the Nardone family of Chicago, at least if they'd lived in the area for any length of time? And Clara had grown up here.

"Um...yes," she said but hesitance laced her voice. What was this woman trying to tell her?

"You know that Tommy, his sister, and their cousins run Gemini Corporation, the biggest up-and-coming security firm in the central part of the country?"

Clara frowned. No, she hadn't known that.

Liz shook her head. "That's ok, not many people do, but it's changed things."

She let that thought roll around a bit, but Liz kept talking. "I only know the details because my brother is marrying into the family. I don't think it's common knowledge yet."

Now Clara was really confused. "Then why are you telling me?"

Liz gave her a long look. "I just thought you might want to know who you're dealing with. And that this," she said holding up a pile of clothes, "isn't even a drop in the bucket for them."

"It still doesn't make sense," she insisted and when Liz gave her a quizzical look, she continued, exasperated, "I tried to kill him!"

Now Liz frowned at her. "Who, Vince?"

Clara hid her face in her hands. "No, Tommy."

There was a beat of silence and then Liz laughed. Clara's head snapped up. She was laughing so hard she'd dropped everything on the floor and was doubled over.

"You," she said pointing, "tried to kill Tommy Nardone, and he's having Vince buy you a new wardrobe while you 'stay' with them?"

Clara nodded dumbfounded by her apparent amusement.

"You must have made quite an impression. Just for that I'm throwing in this," she said holding up a pile of gold shimmering material. "It'll look perfect on you and have Vince tripping over himself."

She blinked as she watched the woman sort through the piles of clothes.

Finally she asked, "What?"

"What, what? It's not the strangest way one of them met their significant other," Liz said with a shrug.

"I'm sorry, you lost me," Clara said, the blood pounding in her ears.

"Well, you like Vince, right? This dress will have him

falling at your feet to do whatever you want. Tommy already approves or you wouldn't be here," Liz pointed out.

Clara opened her mouth to say something, then closed it. "How do you know I like Vince? Isn't that like Stockholm syndrome or something?"

Liz studied her for several long seconds before she shook her head. "No, I don't think that's it. I don't know what happened or what you told him," Liz said, and Clara ducked her head, feeling heat creep up her neck.

Liz gave a throaty chuckle. "Whatever it was it must have been good. Just go after it," she said.

"And what if he just feels sorry for me? What I did was crazy, but I did have a good reason. I don't want his pity," she insisted.

Liz looked toward the shop. "The look on that man's face when he came in here with you? That wasn't pity. That was *I need this woman and I'm hoping buying her works,* which is why he handed over his credit card and not Tommy's, even though the orders are Tommy's."

This was absolutely insane and made no freaking sense. But what if it was true? She'd been just going through the motions trying to get by for so long until all this happened. Was it possible that her attempt at murder might just be the best thing that ever happened to her? She had felt a connection with Vince from the get-go, which had only intensified as he wrung her confession from her. And when she'd given up the information she was certain signed her own death warrant and her fathers by begging him for relief, he'd given it to her and saved her father.

In short, it was crazy. The stuff of stories. Her life had been one blow after another since her mother died. Maybe things were finally starting to turn around?

# TEN

Vince waited in his part of the suite he and Clara were staying in. She'd come home from Liz's shop with an armful of bags. She hadn't seemed excited by the shopping trip, more pensive than anything.

Upon returning to the Nardone house she'd asked him to let her into the adjoining bedroom so she could get ready for dinner. He'd been surprised but agreed. Maybe she wanted to get away from him more than he knew?

He sighed and rubbed a hand over his face. Well, if that were true she would be happy with the news he had for her before they went down to dinner. If she wanted to go, she and her father were free to leave.

He'd been shocked when Tommy had called him to tell him that bit of news. Apparently, Liesel and Jordan had decided to go full frontal on their destruction of the last remaining members of the old guard. Plus, the man who'd contacted and threatened Clara was dead. That hadn't been their doing, but it was just as well. As far as they'd been able to tell, the man hadn't had any other connections besides being a hired thug.

There was no more danger to Tommy, Clara, or her father.

Vince knew he should be happy about that. Instead it made his stomach twist in a painful way. There was a connection between him and Clara. He knew she felt it too. Plus there was the way her body reacted to everything he loved doing. Sure, they'd had an inauspicious start, but she admitted she enjoyed it just as much as he had.

What would she choose? Just because she knew she liked a little pain with her pleasure now, didn't really mean she needed him, but what about the look he saw in her eyes when she thought he wasn't looking back? That was real, he was sure of it.

Still, he had to give her the option.

He had his mind made up and his speech ready when she opened the door, but all of it fled when she stepped into the room. The honey gold dress had a gentle shimmer to it, and it clung to the curves of her body in ways that made him forget his own damn name, let alone everything he needed to tell her.

"What do you think?" she whispered her faintly glossy lips a heady temptation.

"It's beautiful. You're beautiful," he said, sounding breathless.

She gave him a shy smile but lowered her eyes. "Thank you. For the compliment and the dress. I...I really appreciate it."

She stepped in close and looked up at him, her green eyes stunning him so much he didn't even realize what was coming out of his mouth.

"You're free to go," he heard himself say even as his lips crashed down on hers.

She stiffened against him and then relaxed, kissing him back.

When he pulled back, he saw the confusion in her eyes.

"I don't understand. Do you want me to go?" she asked, and he could tell how hard it was for her to look into his eyes as she did so.

"No," he said honestly, "never."

She nodded. "What about my father?"

"He can stay here or go back to the hospital. We have a lawyer working on filing for disability for him, but in the meantime his bills will be covered in full."

That got her attention. "Why?"

That was the million-dollar question, wasn't it?

"I asked Tommy to," he said. "I'll pay him back over time."

She shook her head. "You don't need to do that," she insisted.

"I want to," he said, but he turned away because looking at her was almost too painful. He wanted to ask her, beg her, to stay, but he couldn't. Things had started off all wrong, but he would do what he could to make things right.

"None of this went the right way, and I want you to have a choice," he finished.

He started when he felt her arms wrap around his waist from behind.

"What if it happened exactly how it should? What if I don't want to go? What if being with you, every minute from the moment I first saw you in the bar, was what needed to happen because I didn't feel alive before then?"

Vince closed his eyes. She was saying all the right things, but how could she mean them? The things he'd done in the name of family...were no different than what Rex and

Ari had done to rescue her family. Or what Tommy had done for Bryn. Or what Liesel had done for all of them.

He let out a long, relieved sigh.

"You really want to stay?"

"Only if you want me, and not because you feel guilty," she said, and he heard the steel in her voice.

He turned and gathered her to him, kissing the top of her head. "That's the worst part. I know I should feel guilty, but I can't bring myself to regret a single second of it," he said.

"Good. I don't want you to."

They stood there, just holding one another and Vince felt as though something slipped into place that had always been missing. Yes, he had his work and his family, but he was always apart from them. He might be a Nardone, but only because Tommy's great uncle had approved his bastards using the name. He wasn't really one of them, and yet they treated him as though he was.

Now, he had someone who truly wanted him, for exactly who and what he was. And God help him he was never going to let her go.

"Let's go down to dinner," he said.

"What will you tell them?" Clara asked, her gaze searching his face.

Vince smiled. "The truth, that the woman I love wants to stay with me. They'll understand," he said.

Her eyes lit with laughter. "I imagine they will," she said.

Vince narrowed his eyes. "What did Liz tell you?"

"Plenty," she said with a giggle. "You all seem to have some very interesting ways of meeting the people who love you."

He froze. She loved him too. He'd told her he loved her, so she knew, but he hadn't been expecting her to say it back.

He kissed her again, softly this time, trying to put it into words. She hummed against his lips, and he knew she understood.

# ELEVEN

Clara almost wished they could just stay in their room all night. As crazy as it seemed she loved him, and he felt the same. She felt off balance from how fast life had changed, but that was ok because she also felt whole for the first time as in many years as well.

She'd never been one to shirk responsibility no matter how much of it had come her way, but now, she instinctively knew she wouldn't have to face it alone anymore. So, when she and Vince entered the dining room where everyone else was already waiting, she held her head high.

Being with him made her feel like she could take on anything, even a room full of the family she'd set out to bring down.

Ari spotted her first. "Clara, that dress is gorgeous," she said.

Clara was relieved to see they were all wearing dresses, so she didn't look ridiculous.

Bryn made her way over, her belly bulging. "Looks like shopping went well. How's your father?"

Clara smiled. "He's good, thank you for asking." Her

eyes searched out Tommy. "Thank you for bringing him here," she said meeting his gaze.

Tommy just nodded.

"Are we ready to eat?" an older woman asked from the doorway.

"Just one more minute, Betsy, if you don't mind," Vince said.

Everyone in the room looked at him including the three children. "Clara has agreed to stay," he said, and she felt the entire room relax.

"Really?" Ari all but squealed.

Vince looked at her his eyes bright. "Yeah, for some reason she feels the same about me as I do about her."

Clara saw Liesel sidle over to Tommy and whisper something in his ear. He frowned for a second before a huge smile split his face. He strode across the room and said something to Vince that was too low for her to hear.

He listened and then shook his head, but Tommy spoke a little louder now. "Don't you think you should at least ask and give her the choice?" he said.

Clara looked at them both, her brow furrowed. Ask her what? She'd already agreed to stay.

Vince rolled his eyes, but he turned to her. "Tommy wants to know if you plan on staying for now or forever," he said.

Clara didn't know what to say. Hadn't she already told Vince she felt the same as he did.

"Um...for as long as you want me?" she said trying to come up with a good answer.

"Exactly," Tommy said. "Ask her," he demanded.

Vince heaved a sigh, then with a fluid move he slid to one knee. Clara gaped at him. Wait, what?

"Clara, I'd ask eventually anyway, but this crew are all

getting married Christmas Eve. I know I won't change my mind, so if you want to we can make it a four-way wedding instead of three...Will you marry me? I'm sorry I don't have a ring," he finished chagrin painting his features.

Clara blinked once, twice, and then nodded, whispering, "Yes."

There was a gasp from behind them all and she saw the woman they'd called Betsy.

"Wait just one minute," she said and every single person in the room watched as she hurried from the room.

"What's that all about?" Rex asked, his brow furrowed. They didn't have to wait long to find out. Betsy was back in just two minutes with a small box.

"Your grandmother left this for you, Vince. It was the only thing Enzo Nardone ever gave her besides your father. He couldn't marry her because he had a wife, but he loved her."

She handed him the box, and he opened it. His face was blank for a long minute before he smiled. He turned the box to face her and inside she found a ring with a beautiful fiery opal in it.

"It's not a diamond—" he started to say, but she cut him off.

"It's perfect," she said and meant it.

He slid the ring on her finger. It was a little big, but they could fix that later. She squeezed her hand around it so it wouldn't fall off.

He stood up and kissed her, then pulled her close to him. "I know it's sudden and if you're not comfortable saying no—" he whispered his mouth close to her ear.

She pulled back until she could see his eyes. "I said yes, and I meant it," she said.

His answering smile was breathtaking before he pulled her in close again.

Everyone in the room cheered, but she didn't care. All that mattered were his arms around her and that she never had to give this up.

"Betsy, some champagne I think," Tommy said, and they celebrated the addition of another Nardone wedding all night long.

**How do you pull off Four Christmas Weddings? Find out in the conclusion of the Nardone Family Saga, *Four Weddings At Christmas*.**

## ALSO BY LIA RAE

**Bound Clubs Novels**

Chicago Bound

Atlanta Bound

Paradise Bound

Bound to Be Found

**The Nardone Family Saga**

Bought and Paid For

Caught In the Act

Sought After

Taught a Lesson

Four Weddings at Christmas

**Ranger Valley Ranch Adventures**

The Ranger's Fake Bride

Rescued by the Ranger

The Ranger's Baby

The Ranger's Nanny

www.ingramcontent.com/pod-product-compliance
Ingram Content Group UK Ltd.
Pitfield, Milton Keynes, MK11 3LW, UK
UKHW031259260125
4296UKWH00028B/121

9 798201 333416